W9-DGX-590

MAY   2017

-ump as in jump

Nancy Tuminelly

Consulting Editor Monica Marx, M.A./Reading Specialist

Published by SandCastle™, an imprint of ABDO Publishing Company, 4940 Viking Drive, Edina, Minnesota 55435.

Credits
Edited by: Pam Price
Curriculum Coordinator: Nancy Tuminelly
Cover and Interior Design and Production: Mighty Media
Photo Credits: BananaStock Ltd., Comstock, Corbis Images, Hemera, PhotoDisc, Stockbyte

Library of Congress Cataloging-in-Publication Data

Tuminelly, Nancy, 1952-
    -Ump as in jump / Nancy Tuminelly.
      p. cm. -- (Word families. Set IV)
    Summary: Introduces, in brief text and illustrations, the use of the letter combination "ump" in such words as "jump," "lump," "stump," and "bump."
    ISBN 1-59197-245-0
    1. Readers (Primary) [1. Vocabulary. 2. Reading.] I. Title.

PE1119 .T837 2003
428.1--dc21   2002038636

SandCastle™ books are created by a professional team of educators, reading specialists, and content developers around five essential components that include phonemic awareness, phonics, vocabulary, text comprehension, and fluency. All books are written, reviewed, and leveled for guided reading, early intervention reading, and Accelerated Reader® programs and designed for use in shared, guided, and independent reading and writing activities to support a balanced approach to literacy instruction.

Let Us Know

After reading the book, SandCastle would like you to tell us your stories about reading. What is your favorite page? Was there something hard that you needed help with? Share the ups and downs of learning to read. We want to hear from you! To get posted on the ABDO Publishing Company Web site, send us e-mail at:

sandcastle@abdopub.com

SandCastle Level: Transitional

-ump Words

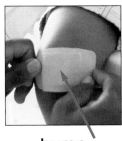

bump

dump

hump

jump

pump

stump

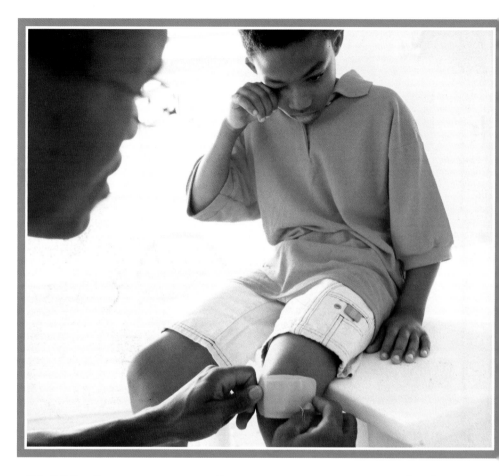

Bill has a bump on his knee.

Birds fly over trash at the dump.

Each camel has a
hump.

Rich can jump very high.

Rod gets a drink from
the pump.

Flowers are growing in
the stump.

A Hump,
a Lump,
and a Bump

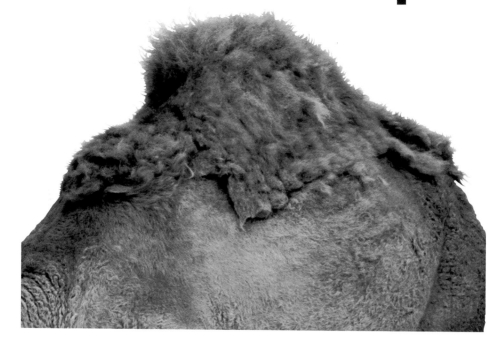

Does a camel have a hump,
a lump, or a bump?

What's in the hump?

Maybe it's air
from a pump!

What if the camel's
hump is just a lump?

13

What if the lump
is a bump the camel got

when it tried to jump
over the stump?

Maybe the camel
fell into the dump.

Maybe that's how
it got the lump.

The camel belongs
to the ump.

The ump is married
to a frump.

The frump does not like
the camel with the hump,
or the lump, or the bump.

The camel is in such
a slump.

It only wants to know,
"do I have a lump,
a bump, or a hump?"

The -ump Word Family

bump	lump
clump	plump
dump	pump
frump	slump
hump	stump
jump	ump

Glossary

Some of the words in this list may have more than one meaning. The meaning listed here reflects the way the word is used in the book.

bump   a lump or swelling

dump   a place where garbage is taken

frump   a girl or woman thought to be dull or plain

pump   a machine used for moving liquids or gases from one place to another

stump   the part of a tree that is left after the tree has been cut down

About SandCastle™

A professional team of educators, reading specialists, and content developers created the SandCastle™ series to support young readers as they develop reading skills and strategies and increase their general knowledge. The SandCastle™ series has four levels that correspond to early literacy development in young children. The levels are provided to help teachers and parents select the appropriate books for young readers.

Emerging Readers
(no flags)

Beginning Readers
(1 flag)

Transitional Readers
(2 flags)

Fluent Readers
(3 flags)

These levels are meant only as a guide. All levels are subject to change.

To see a complete list of SandCastle™ books and other nonfiction titles from ABDO Publishing Company, visit www.abdopub.com or contact us at:

4940 Viking Drive, Edina, Minnesota 55435 • 1-800-800-1312 • fax: 1-952-831-1632